A KID'S GUIDE TO THE X Games

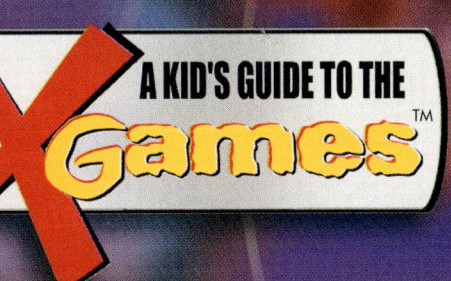

BMX
in the X Games

CHRISTOPHER BLOMQUIST

The Rosen Publishing Group's
PowerKids Press™
New York

For two Xtremely wonderful nephews, Timothy and James

Safety gear, including helmets, kneepads, gloves, shin guards, and elbow pads, should be worn while bicycle stunt riding. Do not attempt tricks without proper gear, instruction, and supervision.

Published in 2003 by The Rosen Publishing Group, Inc.
29 East 21st Street, New York, NY 10010
Copyright © 2003 by The Rosen Publishing Group, Inc.
All rights reserved. No part of this book may be reproduced in any form without permission in writing from the publisher, except by a reviewer.

First Edition

Editor: Nancy MacDonell Smith
Book Design: Michael de Guzman and Mike Donnellan

Photo Credits: Cover, p. 19 © Rob Tringali Jr./SportsChrome USA; pp. 4, 7, 15 © Maura B. McConnell; p. 8 © Stanley Chou/ALLSPORT; pp. 11, © Lutz Bongarts/SportsChrome USA; pp. 12, 21 © Tony Donaldson/Icon SMI; p. 16 © Icon Sports Media.

Blomquist, Christopher.
BMX in the X Games / by Christopher Blomquist.— 1st ed.
    p. cm. — (A Kid's Guide to the X Games)
Includes bibliographical references (p.) and index.
  ISBN 0-8239-6298-9 (lib. bdg.)
 1. Bicycle motocross—Juvenile literature. 2. ESPN X-Games—Juvenile literature. [1. Bicycle motocross. 2. Bicycle racing. 3. Extreme sports.] I. Title.
  GV1049.3 .B56 2003
  796.6'2—dc21

2001006653

Manufactured in the United States of America

Contents

1	What Is BMX?	5
2	The History of BMX at the X Games	6
3	Picking Riders for the X Games	9
4	Some Great X-Games Moments	10
5	Star Riders at the X Games	13
6	The Flatland Event	14
7	The Vert Event	17
8	The Park Event	18
9	A Talk with Ryan Nyquist	20
10	A Look Ahead	22
	Glossary	23
	Index	24
	Web Sites	24

This rider at the 2001 X Games is wearing a helmet, kneepads, and elbow pads to protect him in case he falls.

What Is BMX?

Bicycle stunt riding is a sport in which bike riders do special tricks, called **stunts**, while riding their bikes. The riders do stunts such as jumping over dirt mounds, doing **backflips** in the air, or standing on the bike's seat or handlebars as the bike moves.

Bicycle stunt riding is considered to be an extreme sport because it can be **extremely** risky. Stunt riders wear protective gear to keep themselves from getting hurt. Extreme sports are also action packed, so people call them action sports.

Bicycle stunt riding has two other names, **freestyle bicycle riding** and **BMX**. The letters *BMX* are short for "bicycle **motocross**." The letter *X* stands for the "cross" part of "motocross" because two lines cross when the letter *X* is written.

The History of BMX at the X Games

Every summer and winter, the X Games is held somewhere in the United States. The winter X Games has winter sports that can be done in the snow. The summer X Games has summer sports, including BMX. More than 234,000 people attended the 2001 summer X Games in Philadelphia, Pennsylvania!

Bicycle stunt riding has been a summer X Games sport ever since the very first X Games. Those games took place in Rhode Island in 1995. At the X Games, only men compete in bicycle stunt riding.

At every X Games, **athletes** try to win prizes. These prizes are money and **medals**. In each event, the first-place athlete wins a gold medal. The second-place athlete gets a silver medal. The third-place athlete gets a bronze medal.

BMX athletes do amazing tricks with their bikes. This athlete is making his bike fly through the air!

To ride in the X Games, athletes first have to do well in other competitions. This BMX rider is competing in the Asian X Games, which is one of those competitions.

Picking Riders for the X Games

A few months before the X Games, events called **trials** are held for BMX riders. At the trials, athletes who have never been to the X Games ride for the judges. The two best riders are invited to be in the next X Games.

ESPN, the television station that runs the X Games, picks the judges for the trials and the X Games. Many of the judges used to be extreme athletes.

Other athletes who **qualify** are the five leading scorers from the X Games the year before and the top two riders from each of the X Games that are held in Europe and in Japan. The remaining riders are invited because they did well in other national BMX contests during the year.

Some Great X-Games Moments

One of the most exciting X-Games moments happened in 2000 during the **park event**. There 26-year-old Dave "Miracle Boy" Mirra did his newest trick, a double backflip on his bike. The trick won Mirra his ninth gold medal. This was a new record. Even today nobody has as many X-Games gold medals as Mirra.

In 2001, 22-year-old Bruce Crisman from Oregon rode in his second X Games ever. Crisman's nearly perfect ride in the park event earned him the gold medal. The next day, 21-year-old Stephen Murray from Great Britain did two backflips during the dirt-jumping event. Murray won the gold medal. It was Murray's very first time in the X Games!

Dave Mirra performs a backflip on his bike. Backflips are very difficult to do and take lots of practice.

Dave Mirra, left, and Ryan Nyquist, right, are good friends as well as rivals. Here they stop to talk during the 1999 X Games in San Francisco, California.

Star Riders at the X Games

Dave "Miracle Boy" Mirra is probably the best BMX rider of all time. Every year since 1995, Mirra has won at least one medal at the X Games. He has 10 gold medals and three silver medals.

Ryan Nyquist is another talented rider who has a collection of X-Games medals, one gold, two silver, and three bronze. One of Nyquist's bronze medals was for the park **competition** in 2000, but he won all the others for the dirt-jumping event. In fact Nyquist has won a medal in dirt jumping every year since 1997.

Mirra and Nyquist both live in Greenville, North Carolina. They became good friends while training and touring together.

The Flatland Event

In the flatland event, each athlete rides on a flat cement surface, such as an empty parking lot.

A flatland rider does stunts such as balancing his body as he stands on the bike's **pegs**. To avoid falling over, the rider keeps the bike somewhat still. If the rider's feet touch the ground, he loses points.

Twenty riders participate in a **preliminary round**. The 10 who score the highest ride two more times in a final round. Riders are judged on their style and their stunts.

Flatland riding was not an X-Games event until 1997. In 1997, 1998, and 1999, Trevor Meyer of Minnesota won the gold medal for flatland. Marti Kuoppa of Finland finished first in this event in 2000 and in 2001.

Riders in the flatland event don't do dangerous tricks so they don't always wear safety gear, but it's a good idea to wear a helmet and pads every time you get on your bike.

 Dave Mirra won a gold medal in the vert event at the 2001 X Games in Philadelphia, Pennsylvania. He set a record for the most gold medals won by an X-Games athlete!

The Vert Event

"Vert" is short for **vertical**. A vert rider has between 60 and 75 seconds to coast up and down the sides of a half-pipe. The half-pipe looks like a giant, wooden *U* and is 12 feet (4 m) high. That's as tall as two grown-ups standing on top of each other.

Vert riders fly through the air on their bikes and do flips, turns, spins, and other stunts. Loud music plays during this exciting event. The music helps to stir up each rider's spirits.

Dave Mirra thrilled the crowd at the 2001 vert event by winning the gold medal. It was Mirra's tenth X-Games gold medal. This set a new record for the most gold medals won by a single athlete in X-Games competitions.

The Park Event

The park event takes place on a specially built course that includes **ramps**, J-shaped quarter-pipes, and an area in the middle that looks like a huge, wooden salad bowl. Quarter-pipes look like half of a half-pipe. In the final round of the park event, the 10 best riders get two chances to prove their talent. The riders are allowed to ride anywhere on the course. Like the vert event, the park event usually features a lot of **midair** jumps, flips, and other stunts.

At the 2000 X Games's park event, Dave Mirra won the gold medal and Markus Wilke of Germany took the silver medal. Bruce Crisman won the gold medal at the 2001 X Games. Twenty-two-year-old Alistair Whitton of Great Britain won the silver medal at the X Games that year.

The park event has lots of exciting tricks. This rider is balancing on his handlebars as he jumps through the air.

A Talk with Ryan Nyquist

How do you stay in shape?
I try to ride pretty much every day. That's more than enough of a workout.

What was the 2001 X Games like compared to other X Games?
Inside that stadium, when the crowd cheers, it's **deafening**.... I've never experienced anything like that as far as the crowd being so into it.

You and several other BMX riders all live in Greenville, North Carolina. What is that like?
I think right now we have anywhere from 12 to 15 pros living in that town.... It's awesome [to live there] because you have a lot of the top guys living in one area, so training with them and riding with them only makes you that much better.

Ryan Nyquist ▶

*Did you ever have a **mentor**?*
When I started competing, I would say [my mentor was] definitely Dave Mirra.

*How do you feel about being a **role model** to kids?*
I take it really seriously.... I try to portray a really positive image.

What is your advice for kids who want to try BMX?
Just start with the basics for sure, and make sure you wear all your pads.

Where do you see yourself in five years?
Hopefully on a bike still.

A Look Ahead

Future summer X Games may be in Philadelphia, too. Although there may be some changes made, bicycle riders will probably compete again in all the major bike stunt events, such as dirt jumping, flatland, vert, and park. Downhill BMX, the newest event, was presented for the first time at the summer 2001 X Games. Thousands watched 30 riders race down hills as high as 35 feet (11 m). Twenty-year-old Brandon Meadows from California won the gold medal.

As bicycle stunt riding becomes more popular with young people, new star athletes will appear at the X Games. The wonderful tricks that these athletes do will continue to delight fans all around the world.

Glossary

athletes (ATH-leets) People who take part in sports.
backflips (BAK-flips) Tricks where riders spin upside down in the air.
BMX (BMX) Another way of saying bicycle stunt riding.
competition (kom-peh-TIH-shun) A sports contest.
deafening (DEH-fuh-ning) Very loud.
extremely (ek-STREEM-lee) Very.
freestyle bicycle riding (FREE-styl BY-si-kul RYD-ing) Another way of saying bicycle stunt riding.
medals (MEH-duls) Small, round pieces of metal that are given as awards.
mentor (MEN-tor) A teacher or a coach.
midair (MID-AYR) Happening in the air.
motocross (MOH-toh-kros) A race for bicycles on a dirt course with sharp turns and hills.
park event (PARK ee-VENT) An X-Games event where athletes ride in a specially designed course of ramps and pipes.
pegs (PEHGZ) Short metal tubes that stick out of a stunt bicycle's wheels.
preliminary round (prih-LIH-muh-nayr-ee ROWND) The first part of the competition where the 10 best riders are picked.
qualify (KWAH-lih-fy) To meet the requirements of something.
ramps (RAMPS) Sloping platforms.
role model (ROHL MAH-duhl) A person you want to be like, a hero.
stunts (STUNTZ) Tricks.
trials (TRYLZ) Sports events held before the X Games to test and to find new athletes.
vertical (VUR-tih-kul) In an up-and-down direction.

Index

C
Crisman, Bruce, 10, 18

E
ESPN, 9
Europe, 9

F
freestyle bicycle riding, 5

G
Greenville, North Carolina, 13, 20

J
Japan, 9

K
Kuoppa, Marti, 14

M
Meadows, Brandon, 22
medal(s), 6, 13–14, 17–18
Meyer, Trevor, 14
Mirra, Dave "Miracle Boy", 10, 13, 17–18, 21
motocross, 5
Murray, Stephen, 10

N
Nyquist, Ryan, 13, 20–21

P
Philadelphia, Pennsylvania, 6, 22

S
stunts, 5, 14, 17–18

T
trials, 9

W
Whitton, Alistair, 18
Wilke, Markus, 18

Web Sites

To learn more about bicycle stunt riding and the X Games, check out these Web sites:
www.expn.go.com
www.bmx-style.com

Sunset School Library

FORD CITY PUBLIC LIBRARY
1136 FOURTH AVENUE
FORD CITY, PA 16226